T0171687

A Cat
Named Boy

A Cat Named Boy

JAMES KENSON

PARTRIDGE
A Penguin Random House Company

To order additional copies of this book, contact
Toll Free 800 101 2657 (Singapore)
Toll Free 1 800 81 7340 (Malaysia)
orders.singapore@partridgepublishing.com

www.partridgepublishing.com/singapore

"Bangun Boy! (Wake up Boy!)" The familiar voice of my master woke me up from another deep slumber, just as I was having a wonderful time courting Ms Daisy, the hot Siamese cat. This happened many times recently and I must say Aziz was getting on my feline nerves again. I lifted up my head and gave him a good morning meow greeting, then slid back to my cosy bed. Oh, this comfortable bed of mine is made up of some old clothing of Aziz, padded on a rattan chair. The chair is just next to Aziz's bed, which is made of a simple piece of mattress laid on the cement floor. Me and my master, we live a simple and frugal life together.

"Cepat bagun Boy, jangan tidur lagi. Dah lambat lah kita! (Quickly wake up Boy, no more sleep. We're already late!)" There he'd go hurrying

me again. If you were in my position, you would understand that it's quite an effort to lift up my head to look at the human creatures from where I normally sit or stand. It would cause me prolonged sprain in the neck if I need to lift my head up constantly. This time Aziz didn't wait for my response and lifted my two front legs. He gave me a nose-to-nose kiss, a pleasure I get to enjoy twice a day – always, one in the morning and the other at bedtime. By the way, Aziz could get impatient and wouldn't like waiting too long. So I figured I better get up and leave Ms Daisy behind. Hope to meet you again Ms Daisy; another day, another dream may be?

Aziz had obviously finished his morning routines of dawn prayer, watered the little garden and taken a cold shower. These are the three tasks he never misses before leaving the house every morning. I could tell that he was all dressed up and ready to head for the *mamak* stall – ten minutes' drive down the road. Needless to say, he was craving for the usual breakfast dishes - the all-time Malaysian favourites – *roti canai* and *teh tarik*. Me, I had no choice but to tag along, lest I'd be stranded at home alone the whole day.

Wait, before you start to wonder who the heck am I and what on earth is going on here, let me briefly introduce myself. My master Aziz calls me Boy, though I used to be called Apu. Guess I should be about a year old now, equivalent to the human age of fifteen, which I came to know recently when Aziz related to me a chart of cat's age in human years. As for my looks, there isn't much to shout about. I mean, I wouldn't say I'm good-looking, but neither unattractive like the fat cat next door. I should tell you more about my neighbour Bobo another time. Back to the topic of my looks; with an overall greyish coat of fur interspersed with darker spots, and a pair of green eyes, let's just agree that I'm your ordinary sort of feline albeit a skinny one, a condition I never seemed to overcome from early childhood.

In a way, meeting Aziz had been the most dramatic turn-around event in my life. Prior to that, my late mother and I were fostered by this

Indian family for a short while in a home located within this housing estate, at a place called Sentul. Apparently Sentul was once a thriving railway town, where early Indian settlers worked for the Malayan Railway. Loyalty and employment with the railway would extend to next few generations for many families. Sentul is just about few kilometres outside the city of Kuala Lumpur. Many would claim this place as their homes over the next few decades.

My memory of that early part of life was not pleasant at all, as we were constantly at the mercy of Mr Kumar and his dysfunctional family. For your information, I was born with two other siblings at Mr Kumar's home. Earlier on their second daughter Shalini had persuaded the parents to keep my mother as her pet, the exact period seemed to me ages ago as I had no clear reference to that part of my mother's life.

One thing led to another and my mother was impregnated by a suitor - a father that I never knew. Three kittens were subsequently born into

Mr Kumar's family. On the second month, I realised my two other siblings were given away to Shalini's cousins when they came to know of the new-born kittens. For some time now, I had been wondering why I wasn't given away as well. Perhaps I wasn't that appealing to anyone when they caught the first sight of me, for I was the skinniest compared to my brother and sister. Fortunately, Shalini took a liking on me and decided to keep me as an additional pet in the family, along with my mother. Among the family members, Shalini was a kind hearted soul who treated us with the most loving care. She would gently stroke my head daily when I was a tiny kitten. Indeed she used to call me Apu. On the contrary Shalini's elder sister Malini was a strange and disturbing character. Somehow, Malini would give me this creepy feeling every time she walked by, as I could readily feel her hostility and bad intentions. It was obvious that Malini despised feline creatures like sworn enemies and constantly showed her displeasure over the addition of one more kitten in the family.

She would argue about the rationale of giving us good cooked fish. Through her disgust she would spank us or quarrel constantly with her younger sisters over the burden of keeping two useless cats. On a more positive note, Shalini's mother, Madam Kamala was a wonderful woman with compassionate heart, and she was good cook as well. I still missed the wonderful aroma of curry that Madam Kamala often cooked in those days.

Besides the almost daily commotion arising from sibling rivalry, there was a more serious problem lurking in this family. I very soon discovered that our master Mr Kumar would have this regular bouts of alcoholic excursions with his buddies, at least twice a week. The drinking sessions usually ended up with Mr Kumar piss drunk and his wife and two daughters would be the ones to face the verbal abuse. Thereafter, if the family members were not enough the objects of his outbursts, the cats would become the next targets in his uncontrolled state of madness. Was he physically violent besides the verbal swearing and cursing? You bet! I mean we were regularly getting kicked as if we were obstacles blocking his way! Believe me when I say this; you wouldn't want to be ten feet near Mr Kumar in his state of heavy intoxication.

Now, how did we survive those troubled times, you may ask? For me, I somehow survived by making quick exits to the kitchen or the lavatory at the back of the house as soon as I sensed the roar from Mr Kumar. In so doing, I escaped the dangers of being hurt. Unfortunately, my mother couldn't avoid the assault as she had this wounded hind leg that resulted in her not able to move quickly enough. She died shortly after receiving a full blow during one of those out-of-control Kumarian rampage.

And how did I end up with Aziz anyway? That would be another story to tell. To cut the story short, one week after my mother's death, Shalini realised the chances of me surviving in that household for another day would be too bleak with the increasing bouts of violence. Without much delay she haphazardly wrapped me up with a towel and took me on a bus ride. I could vaguely remember that she left me at the market square not too far from the bus station where we got off. Little did I know, that this would be our first and only trip together, and a farewell trip as well. Upon reaching the market entrance, Shalini cried profusely and pleaded for forgiveness. She kept saying how sorry she was in leaving me alone at a strange place. Me, I was baffled and was trying to make some sense out of the whole situation.

So, there at the Sentul market, I saw Shalini for the last time and realised how similar we were in our physical appearance; she was really a skinny teenager, desperate and helpless over the domestic chaos. With a brief goodbye, I was literally dumped as an orphan by a teenage parent. Now that was a painful lesson, though not the first one, that I learnt about human beings – that they can be cruel and heartless if circumstances require them to make an ultimate decision. You should not expect mercy at all when they made up their minds. It was heart breaking to see the sight of someone I loved and trusted so dearly slowly disappearing from my sight. So it was farewell Shalini, and welcome to the cruel and tough environment of Sentul market.

Very quickly I learnt to survive on whatever I could feed on daily. It was really a place for survival of the fittest, the toughest and the smartest. You would have thought that there were enough thrown away parts of raw fish and meat that could feed the strays roaming the market square. The harsh reality was that the constant hunger and instinct for survival would turn many into scavengers, ever ready to fight for their lives over the limited food supplies. The scenes of wild dogs and cats charging and drawing the first blood would be a daily norm. As the weaker one I couldn't match these bullies by virtue of their size and strength. I would therefore settle for the leftovers. Then there were other smaller creatures such as the rats, birds and flies, ever ready to partake the last bits, if they were fortunate enough to find any remaining scraps. Truly, I witnessed many creatures who were desperate, hungry and destitute, and many premature deaths as well, in the short and horrific period at the Sentul market. Somehow I did get by with the raw stuff, although I never really liked the taste of uncooked fish or meat, for I was brought up on homely cooked food from early childhood.

Despite the traumatic experience, I was not to be left suffering for too long, as fate done me a great favour not long after being deserted by Shalini. My ordeal was shortened when a Malay gentleman showed up at a time when I almost gave up hope on surviving for another day. In fact, I was about to succumb to the never-ending hunger, and was ready for the eventual path towards death like many strays who breathed their last before my eyes.

A miracle descended upon me the day Aziz came to the market to get some fish, shrimps and meat for a community event he was helping with. I could still remember that morning. It was pouring heavily and the market was wetter than usual. Aziz, accompanied by a younger man, were looking for their stuff separately. After he was done with his purchase, Aziz stopped to take a puff by the side of the fish monger stall, amidst the never-ending rain. Me, I was squatting beneath the opposite stall at the side exit when he caught sight of me. Perhaps out of compassion, he took notice and had pity on this skinny cat. He walked towards me and started to stroke my forehead and my lower chin. Now these were the most sensitive parts of my body and I was immediately overwhelmed with intense emotions. I started crying meow, despite being weak and was hardly audible with a feeble voice. I remembered crawling up Aziz' arms with all my strength, in the midst of tremendous sadness. While stroking my forehead, Aziz started to talk to me in some strange language that I couldn't understand. I mean I was an Indian cat called Apu up until then, being raised in an Indian family and understood only Tamil. Now Aziz, what was he talking about? Not long after the other young man returned and Aziz spoke to him for a while and they seemed to have agreed on some arrangement. Very soon I realised Aziz was carrying me in his arm. With an umbrella both of them rushed into a Proton car as quickly as they could, with the downpour heavier by then. I later found out the young man was his nephew Azman, who would come by for occasional visits. From that day onwards, Aziz's home would become my permanent residence, and I soon started to understand the Malay language through my daily interaction with my new master.

With my newly adopted home and Aziz as my new master, you may think that I would quickly erase the unhappy episodes of early childhood and started looking forward to the next phase of my life. Strangely, old memories would creep in some days. The recurring image of my late mother would bring to remembrance of her tenderness and loving care, which reminded me how much I really missed her. I believe she is in a better place now. I heard that there is place called Heaven, and the good people are reserved a place up there when they are done with this world. I also heard that no one would shed a tear in Heaven; it's filled with joy and laughter everywhere. I suppose the good cats ought to be granted a space there like the humans. Yes, with all sincerity, I believe all good creatures should occupy a place in the Heaven as well.

Did I miss the life with Shalini and her family at all? Well, I did initially. The most I missed was the assurance of daily cooked food. And I also missed the wonderful aroma of curry. What I missed most about Shalini was her daily touch and care, and the whisper in my ear, a privilege which I hardly received from Aziz, although he has other ways of showing his affection. Seriously, the nice feeling of human touch is therapeutic and addictive, and will develop into a bonding relationship. Looking back, despite the hardships and misery of constant hunger at the market space, I bear no grudges against Shalini now. Perhaps she had my best interests in mind when she took me out from that house of terror.

Indeed that rainy day was the turning point of my life when I met Aziz. I wonder, would it right to say that Aziz found himself a soul companion in me? In my limited feline intelligence, I gather the happiness and contentment Aziz derived from a loyal pet had been a fulfilment in his search for a meaningful life as well.

I settled into this home at Kampung Baru almost immediately. It is a much bigger house than the previous one at Sentul, although a single storey property as well. I dearly love the ample space and the locality; for the house is relatively quiet and peaceful by comparison. Besides, I get to roam freely without having to worry about my master's temperament. It is a family property Aziz inherited from his parents. The part of house where I spent most of my time, besides our bedroom, would be the porch overlooking the little garden, at the left corner of the front entrance. My favourite pastime would be basking in the morning sun during the weekends, when I am not required to be with Aziz at his workplace.

Most afternoons, after we reached home, Aziz would just let me be on my own, after making sure that my bowl is filled with sufficient cat biscuits for the rest of the day. Me, I would be taking naps at the porch over most lazy afternoons. There are many exotic plants and flowers in this little garden that Aziz had so passionately natured. Oh yes, I like savouring the pungent taste of the *serai*, or lemongrass leaves. You would get a quick high as soon as you chew on them. The awesome feeling is almost like having a puff of cigarette; it sends a smooth sensation right into the body system and you would be in state of elation and happiness beyond description. Apart from that, I love gazing at the variety of flora in their full splendour, particularly the bougainvillea and hibiscus flowers swaying in the gentle breeze, as if dancing in silent meditation. Occasionally some birds and butterflies would make their presence and that would be like colourful embellishment to a picturesque canvas. It seemed strange that the urge to catch those flying creatures had never occurred to me, as for unknown reasons I would prefer to sit and watch, and enjoy those beautiful creations of God. Indeed, these would definitely be the tranquil and peaceful moments I look forward to each afternoon.

Alas, my daily afternoon siesta would sometimes get interrupted by a neighbour who would come uninvited. This disruption to the quiet and serene afternoons which I guarded so dearly had been caused frequently by one inconsiderate cat. I am speaking about Bobo the elderly cat next door of course. Predictably, Bobo would drop by most afternoons to search me out, as he seemed to know my schedules very well.

"Hey young man, how was your day with Aziz today?" This would be a standard opening line from Bobo. His limited range of vocabulary reminded me of a parrot I befriended recently at the coffee shop; always a standard line of greeting, so unsurprising that would bore me to death. Somehow I would bear with the inconvenience out of respect for an elderly cat. The thing about Bobo is that he had this tendency to boast, mostly about the many conquests during his younger days. He would talk about the great adventures and romances he had and how many females he courted in his prime. I could sort of understand his predicament and therefore would just entertain his intrusions to the best of my patience and tolerance. I suppose senior folks tend to reminisce about good old days, back to a period of their life that remind them of the happiness long gone by. How sad that they need the constant memory play backs to reassure them that they are staying alive and relevant?

It's puzzling to me that if at all Bobo was living such a flamboyant and exciting life, how on earth did he end up as an old and lonely fat cat, living a boring life in this quiet neighbourhood? For obvious reasons, I consciously reminded myself not to inquire anything about Bobo's past, or even his current affairs, lest I would get into unnecessary and long winded conversations. A normal situation would be that after the usual pleasantries, Bobo and I would end up sitting next to each other on the porch, silently enjoying the afternoon bliss. Oh yes, it's a blessed life for us cats, to be able to laze around and do absolutely nothing, unlike the human creatures with their never-ending pursuits, something beyond my limited feline understanding.

With fairness and sincerity, I consider Aziz a peaceful and easy going person, based on his laidback and carefree character. Humble in mannerism and gentle in his speech, he would be probably in his early forties now. He is tanned and slightly built with a face that is rather haggard and wrinkled; I gather mostly probably the result of past substance abuse. He seemed determined to forget the past and put all those histories behind. I sensed Aziz would prefer not to revisit the topic at all. In fact, he would get uneasy whenever someone inquire of his younger days. As far as I know, he has never married. He makes his livelihood as cobbler at a five foot way corner of a coffee shop, in downtown Kuala Lumpur.

On normal days, after the working hours, Aziz would be spending time with his buddies at a football field not too far from our home. He and his friends would have their game of light football most evenings and I would be left on my own at home, free to do whatever I like; though I would be sleeping most of the late afternoons. By the way, we cats just love spending most of our day sleeping, whenever we find the opportunity to indulge in this favourite past time.

There is a hidden talent of Aziz that not many people know of, and I had the privilege to witness regularly; that he plays the guitar very well. Most nights, after dinner, Aziz would pick up his acoustic guitar and start to play his vast repertoire of slow rock numbers. If his nephew Azman is around for visit, he would tap on the table to provide the constant beat and the two would sing their favourite tunes away. Although his skills on the instrument are well honed, I can't say the same about Aziz's singing. It's obvious that one can't have too many talents in one's lifetime. My favourite tunes would be 'Isabella' and 'Soldier of Fortunate'. Indeed, each time they played these numbers, I would place my paws on Aziz's thighs, a gesture for encore!

I found out later that, through some old photographs that Azman showed me about his uncle, that Aziz was once a guitarist of a rock band. Along the journey to stardom, the band members got themselves into trouble with the law and that ushered the early career demise for this group of promising young talents. There were other interesting stories as well but Aziz would quickly put a stop to the conversation whenever he sense the nephew overstepped the boundaries.

Something about Azman the nephew. He works as a caricature artist in the Central Market, a place where many artists congregate. Azman is an accomplished artist and his skills in caricature drawing would earn a decent living. He even drew a portrait of me and called it 'A Cat Named Boy'. Aziz liked the drawing so much that he proudly framed it and had it nicely hanged in the living room as a decoration piece. It's really an honour, that my portrait is being displayed almost like an object of reverence in our home. On some weekends Aziz would take me along when he visits Azman and his artistic pals at the Central

Market. They would spend the whole afternoon just enjoying each other's company, chatting away and having the regular *teh tarik*, a favourite Malaysia past time. I noticed most of the pals have the common traits; relaxed, laid-back and have time for each other. By comparison, we cats are loners and we guard our private space very dearly, and I suppose there is no way we can do anything to change this cat nature of ours.

Among the pals, Aziz would be the one who takes the initiative to put refreshments on the table whenever they meet. I would see him busy serving everyone, never once tired of showing hospitality. Oh yes, Aziz is what I would consider a caring and selfless human being. He was my saviour once and now he is my good master. I hope we will never part until the day either one of us leaves this planet - till death do us part!

"*Cepat masuk kedalam bakul, Boy* (Quickly get into the basket, Boy)." Aziz motioned for me to get into the front carriage of his Suzuki motorbike. Thus began another day of routine for me and my master. It was about 7.00am and the morning crowd of office workers were already busy congregating along the road leading to the bus station at Jalan Sultan Abdullah. Me, I really enjoyed this morning ride with Aziz. Amidst the cool fresh air and morning breeze, the gradual roar of the busy traffic welcomed another hectic day for many in this big capital city.

"*Hello mamak, kasi biasa punya: telur setengah masak dua biji dengan satu teh tarik* (Hello mamak, give me the normal stuff: two half-boiled eggs with one *teh tarik*)." Aziz ordered his normal breakfast, a la carte Malaysian style.

"*Okay, sikit jam boss* (Okay, a little while, Boss)." Replied the stall owner. He must be doing good business, judging from the steady stream of customers making their way to the limited seats. With the full breakfast crowd and one young helper, mamak was struggling to meet the demands of morning customers from all walks of life; they come in different shapes and sizes, each ready to savour their favourite choices of breakfast.

While waiting for the orders to be served, Aziz opened up the wrapping of a packet of *nasi lemak* and started scooping on the coconut-milked rice stuffed with fried anchovies and chilli paste. This would be the part of the day he enjoys his utmost pleasure. Besides the sumptuous food, Aziz would indulge in his reading of *The Star*, while catching up with his group of breakfast companions. Most of the conversations would centre on local politics and their anti-government rhetoric. Me, I don't usually take my breakfast this early. By the way, my breakfast dish would be ready only at the coffee shop when Aziz starts his business there. Besides,

I enjoy eavesdropping over the conversations of Aziz and his pals. I would be startled at their endless complaints and secretly laughed at their inability to do anything significant except the constant curses and criticisms. They talked as if the government of the day would crumble amidst all the cracks and divisions within, as well as the ever increasing dissent from the ordinary folks across the country. Lately there had been talks that foreign agents were involved in exposing the ever scandalous deeds and cover ups by those high up in the corridors of power. All these angsts and frustrations somehow kept the ordinary folks alive. From feline's point of view, I find these negative energy and constant fury difficult to comprehend. By contrast, cats are generally peace loving animals and we tend to mind our own business. We don't need support for our opinion or our philosophy in life. I wonder could it be that we are selfish creatures after all?

Breakfast would normally last half an hour or so and we would head towards downtown Kuala Lumpur, where Aziz starts his daily business routine at about 8.00am. It's a corner coffee shop by the bend of old Klang bus station. Aziz would park his motorbike at an open-air car park nearby. It would cost him one *Ringgit* a day. He would then carry me on his left arm, while his right hand clutching a wooden tool box, with a sling bag hanging over his shoulder. Thereafter, we would proceed towards the shop which is a mere few minutes' walk from the car park. On route we would pass by this Indian temple as it is located adjacent to the street towards our destination. The smell of incense from the temple would fill the air. It would bring back memories of my short stay with Shalini and her family. During this daily routine, I would immerse myself in this scent of mystical India, infused with the sound of prayers by the morning worshippers; while watching the flock of birds chirping away at the roof top of the temple. The spiritual elements surrounding this temple must have a special meaning and effect on the birds, for there appear to be constant stopovers by different species, almost like fulfilling vows or performing their pilgrimages at this holy shrine.

"*Jangan lari ke sini sana, duduk diam dekat kotak, Boy* (Don't run here and there, sit quietly near the box, Boy)." Aziz reminded me not to roam further away from the shoe stall. He tended to worry and would insist that I sit still when he starts to get busy with works. Indeed I spent a lot of my time lazing on my favourite spot next to Aziz, while at the same time observed the activities and happenings around the coffee shop throughout the day.

The variety of tools that a cobbler rely on for his trade had never ceased to amaze me. Within Aziz's wooden tool box you can find items such as scissors, hand blades, big needles, nails, iron nail pullers, pliers and iron shoe stand. Then there are tins of glue, shoe polish, as well as sheets of leather and PVC leather that are used for patching the broken shoes or bags.

Some mornings, as soon as we had set up the stall, you would find customers already waited for a while, eager to send in items that need repair. Generally Aziz would indicate to customers a suitable time to return for collection, if the items are not urgently required. For those who need to have the repair instantaneously, Aziz would then suggest that they have their breakfast or a cup of beverage while waiting for the repair. A typical shoe repair would take half an hour the least. On a good day, you could expect more than a dozen or so customers; whereas on a rainy day or on the eve of public holidays, you would be lucky to attain a fraction of that business volume. Come rain or shine, we close business at about 3pm each day.

Aziz is really a skilful and well-liked cobbler, noticeably from how he would effortless stitch and glue all kinds of shoes or bags brought to his stall. The normal peak hours for his business would be around lunch, where many office workers of both sexes would start to roll in. Some regular customers seemed to have more than few pair of shoes, which seemed luxurious in my opinion. Indeed I witnessed many repeat customers who are just like old friends to Aziz. Over the years they had developed a kind of trust and relationship with their favourite cobbler, and would not haggle over the price that he charges. Some customers would even send hampers before the festival of *Hari Raya*, as appreciation to their favourite cobbler.

In the course of spending most of the working hours with Aziz, I suppose no other felines would have had the opportunities to witness the many different types of shoes in their entire cat life. There were flat soles and high heels, all sorts of sneakers, sandals, occasionally boots and loafers, slippers, and some would even bring their broken sling bags, sports bags and luggage bags for repair. Also, by tagging along with Aziz and spending time with him daily, I learnt much about human creatures, just by watching and musing over the characters and behaviour of different customers that visited the shoe stall or the coffee shop daily.

The coffee shop is run by this lady with a simple name of Ah Sou. Nobody actually knows or cares to find out about her real name; but everyone calls her Ah Sou, which I came to know a little later that it's an affectionate term in Cantonese, similar to 'madam'. Now, Ah Sou is quite an interesting character in my feline opinion. She must be in her fifties and her overall appearance to me is no different from a heavy chunk of meat, albeit a cute one. She talks fast and loud and sends shivers to her team of Burmese workers every time she raises her voice, especially when the crowds start to pile in and the orders not being served timely. But beneath this rough and fearsome character, there lies a gentle and caring motherly figure which I grew to appreciate more each day. In fact, I began to witness the softer side of Ah Sou as I spent more time at the coffee shop.

Ah Sou took over the running of the coffee shop since her late husband died of a sudden heart attack some years ago. Widowed with two teenage children, Fen Fen, the eldest daughter and Meng Meng the younger son, she had no choice but to step up, took the helm and continue with the family business. The coffee shop is a double-storey building left by the deceased parents of her late husband, as an ancestral home and inheritance, just like many early Chinese migrants would do in those days. It seemed like a common path taken by the early Chinese migrants in this country, where they would invest in a shop lot after they had accumulated enough wealth through hard work and diligent savings. They would become shop owners and landlords and would customarily sub-divide the property into few smaller denominations and let out to smaller eatery business owners. These tenants would in turn run their specialty food stalls by paying a fixed monthly rental. While sub-letting of space, the shop owner would keep the most lucrative part of the business in supplying the beverage of hot and cold drinks. Prior to the influx of foreign workers from countries such as

Indonesia, Myanmar and Nepal, the shop used to employ older local Chinese folks, and they were not cheap in their salaries comparing to the newer migrant workers. With the arrival of cheaper foreign workers some years ago, Ah Sou's two children were spared from helping with the family business and the daughter Fen Fen had since married and moved overseas. Meng Meng is grown-up young man now. He works as an IT engineer with a multinational company and had long ago declared that he would have no part in carrying the family business tradition. He does drop by occasionally when he is around that part of the town but hardly stays any longer. Ah Sou, like any mother, would nag the son about almost everything and anything.

If I regard Aziz as my father figure, it wouldn't be inappropriate to say that Ah Sou is like a mother figure to me - period. One the first day that she caught sight of me, it was obvious that she had an immediate fondness towards this skinny little cat. I was like the son she missed so much and all her affection was showered upon me. I can still remember whence she first carried me in her arms and inquired all about this little kitten from Aziz. There was an incident whence Aziz almost quarrelled with Ah Sou over her unintentional but good gesture to feed me a piece of luncheon pork meat, which caused Aziz to confront her due to the impurities of non-halal food. From then on, I would be given a piece of fried *ikan mabong* (mabong fish) each day, around 11am. Ikan mabong is a staple fish for most Malaysians. This is an arrangement Ah Sou made with the *chap fan* (mixed rice) stall owner next door, five times a week, except Saturdays and Sundays. So after much craving of cooked fish, it was like a dream come true when I started to have the constant supply of this dish almost daily again. Isn't it amazing how an unassuming cat get to reverse his fortune through having a new master?

There are other interesting people that I would come into contact regularly at the coffee shop. Apart from Ah Sou the landlord cum beverage supplier, Ah Keong the wanton noodle guy would be the stronger anchor tenant from the volume of customers that patronise almost non-stop from morning until the peak hour at lunch. He recently got married and his wife started to help out in the business, besides the Indonesia maid helper. Then there is the chicken rice seller Fei Loh. He has a Burmese lady to help deliver the order. He is doing good business as well although the crowd seems to come in for chicken rice dishes mostly during the lunch hour.

Ah Sou must be the biggest gainer of all the customers that flow in and out of the coffee shop; you can possibly tell when you see her grinning constantly, with the sound of cash register ka-chinging through her ears. It is common that most customers would order a drink, either hot or cold beverage while waiting for the meals to be served, although their main order may be a bowl of wanton noodle or a plate of chicken rice.

On the far corner there is this Indonesian lady Maria who trades her egg tart and pastries. But she could be inconsistent as I noticed her stall would not be opened daily like the rest. And finally, the lottery ticket seller Velu who would come by the coffee shop few times a day. He would routinely go around each table, selling hope to those on a never-ending pursuit and a dream to hit the jackpot, and in the process become an instant millionaire. The variety of Chinese dialects that Velu commands is simply amazing. Admittedly, I admire his talents as my own monosyllable meow would be really negligible in comparison.

Funny though, I discovered that most days, while in the coffee shop, my vision of the world around me would be all sorts of legs! And there are legs with many different types of shoes, busy making their way across, as well as in and out of the coffee shop. Unless I lift my head up to have a closer look of those who are near me, I would basically see many legs passing by daily. Through this, I noticed the almost constant hurry in the surroundings, where everyone seemed busy trying to get their priority and things done. From these observations, I came to a conclusion that life tends to be busy for most of the human creatures. They somehow had to be busy to make a living or making ends meet. The daily rush and struggles seemed endless and they hardly had the luxury of slowing down to smell the flowers or feel the gentle breeze; a pleasure and leisure that Bobo and myself get to enjoy daily.

In comparison, life is rather blissful for a cat like me. Unlike humans, we felines don't need to get busy at all to make a living. As a matter of fact, we would have had it made once we found a good master. In this context, I am one of those who had obviously made it, though not without some hardships and near-death experience during the first few months with the Kumarian family, and the subsequent desolation at the market place. In essence, life had turned around for the better and I must be grateful to have gained favour from the Creator above, and the affection and care of my master Aziz.

"Okay, cukup Boy, pergi tidur. Dah malam, jangan main lagi (Okay, enough Boy, go to sleep. It's late at night, no more playing)." After the nightly routines of songs and plays, Aziz signalled that it was time for bed. Once we had the nose-to-nose kiss, he put me on the rattan chair and patted my head again. It would be the end of another day for us. The affection shown by Aziz, although seemed controlled and restrained in comparison to those I used to receive from Malini, are nevertheless sufficient for me. I came to understand that males and females express their emotions differently, from the daily observations of human behaviour throughout my brief yet memorable experiences in life so far.

It's time for bed and I'm thinking would I be meeting Ms Daisy again in a dream tonight?

Or perhaps I may dream of my late mother. These would be wonderful encounters that I look forward to, but you never know. For lately I had been having the recurring dream of a prolonged life at the Sentul market. You can imagine how horrifying it would be to revisit that godforsaken place again! So, I am toying with this idea of saying a sincere prayer, something that I picked up from observing Aziz's daily prayer routines. Perhaps the good Lord can spare me from this possible nightmare, and instead bless me with a sound and peaceful sleep? Yes, perhaps the good Lord in His mercy may just grant me this humble request as I pray. Amen.

Printed in the United States
By Bookmasters